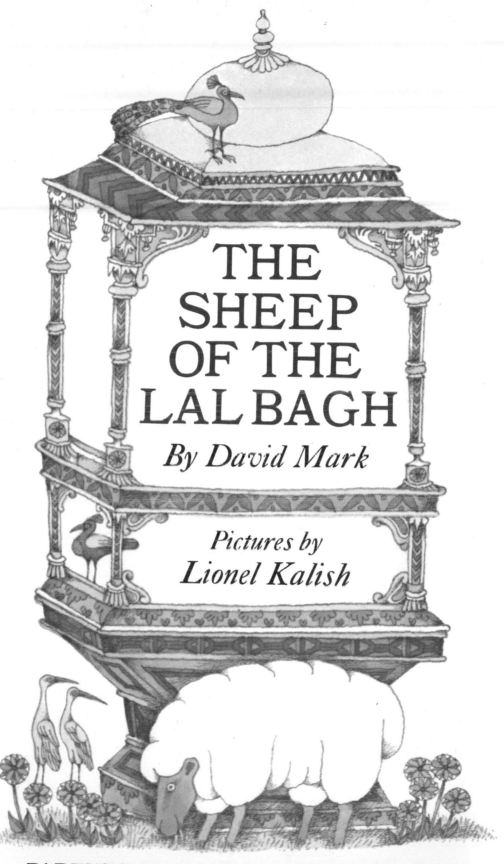

# THE SHEEP OF THE LAL BAGH

*By David Mark*

*Pictures by*
*Lionel Kalish*

PARENTS' MAGAZINE PRESS / NEW YORK

TO JEANNE WITH LOVE

In a little city in the heart of India there was a big park called the Lal Bagh.

From miles around, the people, who worked very hard,
came to the Lal Bagh to relax and enjoy themselves
on holidays. There is a lot of hard work in India,
but there are also a lot of holidays.

They came to see the big white petals of the lotus flowers
opening and closing in the pond. And the rubbery plants
and stickly plants and curly plants in the glass house.
And the flame-of-the-forest trees that dotted the sky with orange.
And the water in the fountain making rainbow splashes.

**B**ut most of all they came to see the lawn mower.

This was not a very new or modern lawn mower. It did not cut the grass very quickly. In fact, it was not a machine at all. It was a sheep. His name was Ramesh.

**E**very morning, just at sunrise, he started at one corner of the lawn. He bent his head and cropped the grass close to the ground.

On holidays, his mowing was very special.
On the solemn holidays he mowed in large circles
that got smaller and smaller until he reached the middle.

On the happy holidays he started at the center and mowed out to the corners and the sides until the lawn was shaped like a star. Ramesh took a lot of pride in his work.

His holiday mowing took a long time because there were many interruptions. The men came over and patted him on the back. They grinned and said, *Ramesh!* The women came over and rubbed his head. They smiled and said, *Ramesh!* And the children came over and got on his back, and as he took them for slow jogging rides, they laughed and shouted, *Ramesh!*

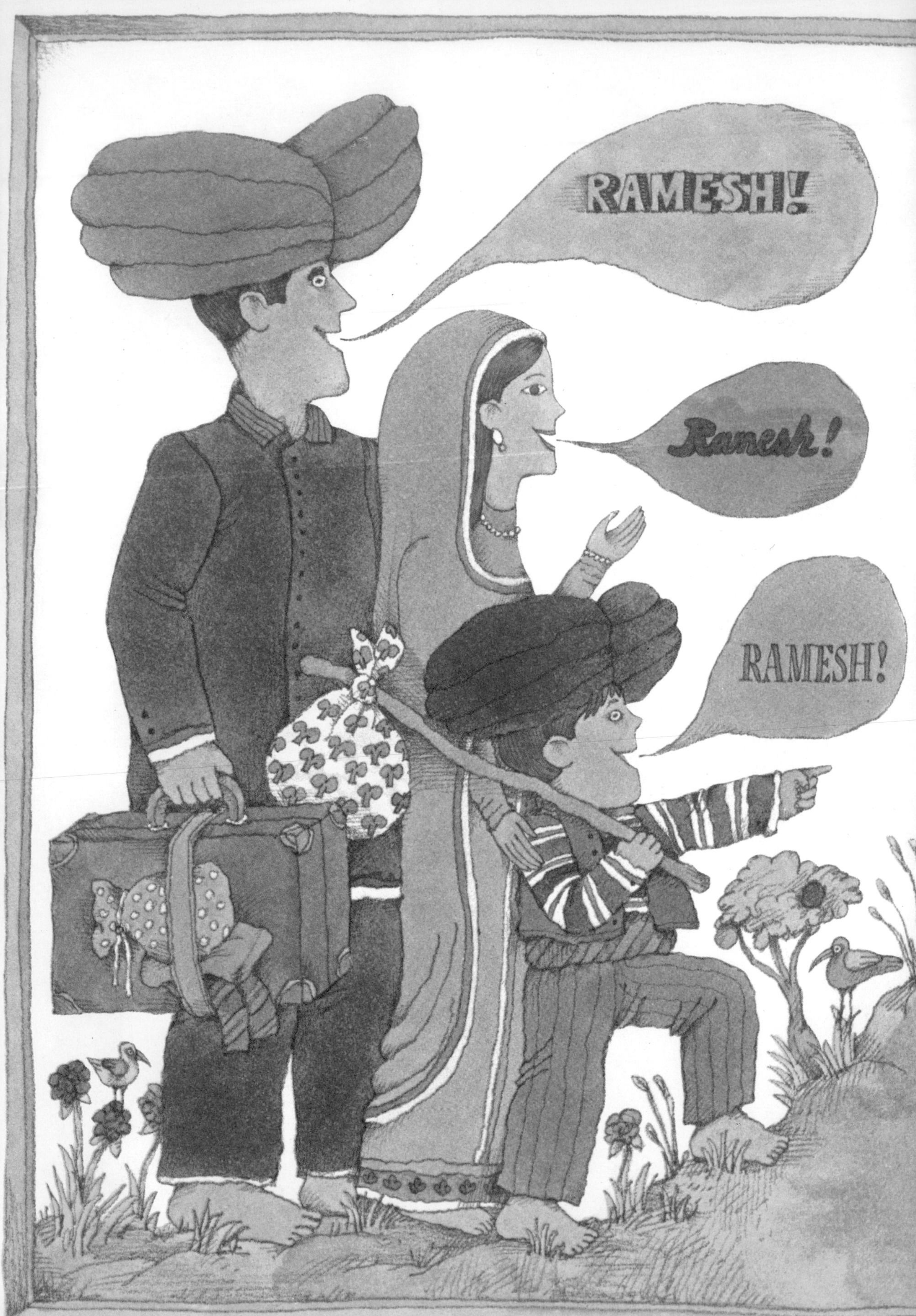
RAMESH!
Ramesh!
RAMESH!

Rajendra was one of these men, and his wife Kamala was one of these women, and their son Krishna was one of these children. They had lived on a farm in the country, but they had lost their land and had come to the city. The Lal Bagh reminded them of the country, and Ramesh reminded them of their farm. It seemed to make them all feel better just to say, *Ramesh!*

**B**ut the mayor of the little town in the heart of India was not satisfied with his lawn mower. He called the parkmaster.

**W**e must have a machine to mow the lawn," he said.
"But we can't afford it," replied the parkmaster.
"The people want to be proud of their city," cried the mayor.
"They will pay for it."

The people paid for the machine. Rajendra and Kamala
and Krishna contributed their few pennies, too.

They wanted to be proud of the city, as long as they had to live in it. They did not understand the machine was going to take Ramesh's place.

The first time Ramesh saw the machine cutting the grass he turned, and with his head down he walked out of the park, up a hill and out of sight.

**H**e joined a flock of grazing sheep. They did not understand why he ate the grass in circles or star shapes. And they never knew why, every now and then, he raised his head and stood looking down the hill with big sad eyes.
So they just went about their munching and left him alone.

On the next holiday Rajendra and Kamala and Krishna, and a lot of other people, went to the Lal Bagh as usual. They enjoyed the lotuses in the pond and the plants in the glass house, the water in the fountain and the orange blossoms of the trees. But when they got to the lawn there was no Ramesh. Only a machine.

They could not pat a machine, or rub a machine's head,
or climb on a machine's back and ask it for a ride.
So little by little the people stopped coming to the park.
Workdays or holidays, nobody came.

The mayor called in the parkmaster.
"Where are the people?" he cried.
"They don't come since Ramesh left," said the parkmaster.
"We must find that sheep!" roared the mayor.

A committee was appointed to find Ramesh. But a committee really can't tell one sheep from another, so they could not find him.

Then Rajendra and Kamala and Krishna went up the hill
to look for Ramesh. Rajendra thought he could recognize
Ramesh from the way his woolly body felt, and Kamala thought
she could recognize him by the look in his eyes. So Rajendra
started at one end of the flock, patting, and Kamala started
at the other, looking. They could not seem to find Ramesh.
But Krishna noticed one sheep off by himself, eating
the grass in neat circles around a banyan tree.

Ramesh!" he cried as he jumped on the sheep's back.
"A ride, Ramesh, a ride!" and that was how Ramesh
came back to the Lal Bagh.

N ow the machine mows the lawn, very straight and very fast,
only on workdays. Rajendra and Kamala and Krishna
and all the other people feel proud that their park
is up-to-date this way. Of course they don't get a chance
to see the machine very often because they are working.

About the only one who sees it is Ramesh. He does not mind now, and he does not hang his head, because on the holidays *he* is the lawn mower.

When he is not having his back patted by men like Rajendra, or his head rubbed by women like Kamala, he makes solemn circles in the grass between the green plants in the glass house and the white lotuses in the pond. And when he is not taking children like Krishna on his back and giving them little rides, he eats happy stars in the grass between the rainbow splashes of the fountain and the orange blossoms of the trees.